Meet Lazy, the British Bulldog toy.
Join him on his exciting new adventure
at Kenilworth Castle as he dreams
of becoming King of the Castle.

Lazy, King of the Castle

By

Ann Evans & Robert D Tysall

Lazy could not believe his ears!
Daddy said he would take him to an
ancient castle.
Lazy knew that Kings and Queens
lived in castles.
Maybe he would see a King or a Queen!

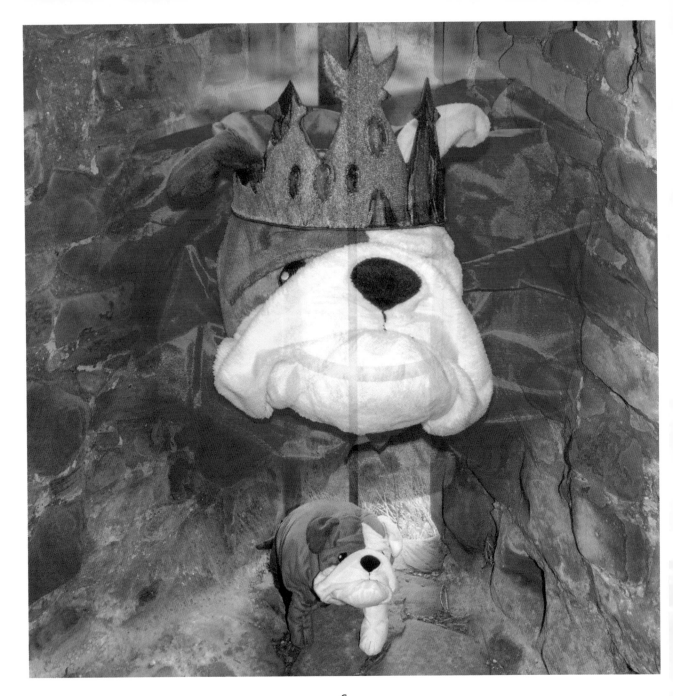

Maybe he could become King for a day!

King Lazy!

Lazy's tail wagged happily all the way there.

Lazy could not believe his eyes.

The castle was so **big** with mighty

towers and sturdy brick walls.

Lazy thought it was very grand, very

exciting... and very orange.

"The bricks are made of sandstone,"

said Daddy. "That's why they are orange,

the colour of sand."

"So, is it a sandcastle?" Lazy asked.

"Ho ho! Lazy," laughed Daddy.

"No, this is a real Medieval castle."

The castle stood proudly at the top of
a grassy green hill.
Daddy said this was Kenilworth Castle.
Many famous Kings had lived here -
King John and King Henry.
But never a King Lazy – until today!
Lazy was so excited that he scampered to
the top of the hill and daydreamed
about being King!

Hurrah! For King Lazy!

As King Lazy daydreamed, he imagined
himself in a fine crown, his red cape blowing
in the breeze.

He was armed with a sword and shield.

And everyone bowed to him -

King Lazy.

The finest King in the whole of the land.

Daddy said Kenilworth Castle was very, very old – 900 years old!
It was so old that some of the walls had fallen down. And some parts of the castle did not even have a roof.

Lazy hoped Daddy did not think **he** had broken the walls and the roof.
Daddy laughed. "Ho ho! Lazy.
Of course not! These are the famous castle ruins!"

They explored the castle ruins and Lazy found some huge gates.

"Knights in shining armour rode through these gates, long ago," said Daddy.

Lazy imagined guarding the gates from invaders.

Armed with his sword and shield, King Lazy was the bravest King in all England.

As King of the castle, Lazy sat on a fine throne. But it was made of hard wood and was not very comfortable! Lazy decided it would be more fun playing in the castle grounds. Sitting on a hard throne was a bit boring – even if you were King.

Outside, Lazy could not believe his luck!

He found a new friend – Snooty Bear.

Snooty Bear wore a golden harness.

He told Lazy that many years ago, the

gardens here at the castle had been

made especially for the

Queen of England - Queen Elizabeth I.

Lazy stood on the balcony and looked out over the Castle garden.
It was filled with flowers, potted plants, statues and even an aviary full of beautiful birds.

Together, Lazy and Snooty Bear daydreamed of Queen Elizabeth I enjoying the beautiful garden.

Then, saying goodbye to Snooty Bear, Lazy explored the castle some more.

There were lots of steps and stairways.

Lazy could not believe his luck again!

He found two smooth banisters to slide down.

"Oh, Oh! Lazy No!" called Daddy.

"Don't slide down the banisters!"

But as King of the castle, Lazy could do whatever he wanted!

WHEEEEEEEEEEEEEEE!!!

Lazy slid faster and faster down the banister.

His cape flew one way.

His crown flew another.

And his ears flapped

as the wind whistled by.

WHOOOOOOSH!!!!!

CRASH! BANG! WALLOP!

Lazy came to a sudden stop!

His crown slid over his eyes.

His ears flipped and flopped.

And his eyes went all of a wobble!

"Oh!! Lazy!" cried Daddy.

Lazy was a bit worried.

Was he in big trouble for

sliding down the bannister?

What if they locked him away in

the dungeon?

That would not be much fun!

Lazy started to think....

Maybe being a King in a cold, draughty castle was not such a good idea after all.

Lazy thought of his nice warm house.

And his nice warm bed.

And a nice, tasty treat to eat...

"Ho ho! Lazy, are you hungry?" asked Daddy.
And before Lazy could believe his eyes,
Daddy gave him a lovely cream scone
with strawberry jam.

It was a treat fit for a King!

We hope you have enjoyed Lazy's adventure at the castle.
Watch out for more fun stories with loveable Lazy.

About the Authors

Children's writer, Ann Evans, loves to write mysteries and adventure stories. She often writes about animals but she has never met one like Lazy before. Ann says he was good fun to work with and she's looking forward to writing about his next adventure.

Photographer, Rob Tysall, can be found at Tysall's Photography. Rob often takes photographs of dogs, cats and lots of other animals. He says that Lazy is not at all like his name. He's always full of beans and up to mischief.

Websites for more information:
www.annevansbooks.co.uk
https://www.facebook.com/tysallphotoandimage

Have you read these Lazy Adventure books?

Lazy's First Christmas

Lazy at the Garden Centre

Lazy at the British Motor Museum

Watch out for more adventures with Lazy.

Follow Lazy on Facebook:

https://www.facebook.com/AdventuresOfLazy/

If you enjoy Lazy's adventures, why not ask a grown up
to leave a review so other young readers can meet Lazy too.

Thank you.

COLOUR IN LAZY'S PICTURE

He can be any colour you want!

Printed in Great Britain
by Amazon